THE STORY BEHIND THE WATTERSON HOUSE

BY CHARLIE HART

ILLUSTRATED BY SHANE L. JOHNSON

An Imprint of Penguin Random House

CARTOON NETWORK BOOKS
Penguin Young Readers Group
An Imprint of Penguin Random House LLC

Photo credits: page 1, 56, 58: (floor) © malven57/iStock/Thinkstock; page 4–5: (carpet) © fatchoi/iStock/Thinkstock, (wall) © lookwai/iStock/Thinkstock; page 16–17: (grass) © Dmitry Kosterev/Shutterstock; page 43: (ceiling, wall) © OceanFishing/iStock/Thinkstock, (floor) © luoman/istock/Thinkstock; page 51: (roof) © Comstock/Stockbyte/Thinkstock; (inside gutter) © comstock; (drainpipe) © Amy Walters/iStock/Thinkstock; page 54: (ceiling) © lookwai/iStock/Thinkstock.

Published in 2016 by Cartoon Network Books, an imprint of Penguin Random House LLC, 345 Hudson Street, New York, New York 10014. Printed in the USA.

ISBN 978-0-8431-8346-7 10 9 8 7 6 5 4 3 2 1

The Sweater

Gumball's sweater was full of holes. There were stains on the front, and threads stuck out all over it like stray hairs. It was always getting snagged on furniture and bushes.

One morning, as Gumball was pouring milk onto his breakfast cereal, Gumball's mother, Nicole, saw Gumball's belly button peeking through a hole in the sweater.

"You can't go to school like that," she said.

"Why not?" asked Gumball.

"I can see your belly button."

"I like my belly button," said Gumball.

"Everyone does," said Darwin. "It's very handsome."

"Yes," said Nicole, "you have a very nice belly button, Gumball, but the entire world should not be able to see it through a hole in your sweater. You need a new one."

"A new belly button?" Gumball asked, alarmed.

"Where would we buy one of those?" wondered Darwin.

Nicole sighed. "No, Gumball. Not a new belly button. You need a new sweater."

"But this is my favorite sweater," said Gumball.

"It's your only sweater," said Nicole.

"It's my lucky sweater!" said Gumball, crossing his arms. As he did, there was a loud *riiiiip-**POP!*** as his elbow tore through a hole in his sleeve and bumped Darwin's arm. The spoonful of cereal Darwin was trying to put in his mouth ended up in his **eye**.

Across the table, Anais, Gumball's little sister, shook her head. "Doesn't look very lucky to me," she said.

"We're going to the mall today," said Nicole. "I'm getting you a new sweater, Gumball, and that is that."

Gumball didn't want a new sweater, but he went to the mall with Nicole anyway. Darwin and Anais came along, too. When they got to the department store, Darwin and Anais ran straight to the boys' department and began pointing out all the sweaters that they liked.

"These sweaters have sparkles on them!" said Darwin.

"These sweaters have airplanes on them!" said Anais.

"*These* sweaters are the ones we can afford," said Nicole. She flipped through a rack of plain sweaters, checking sizes. She picked one out and handed it to Gumball.

"There's nothing special about this sweater," he said.

"Try it on, please," said Nicole as she led the way to the changing rooms.

The changing-room attendant asked, "How many items?"

"Just one," said Gumball glumly. "One plain, boring sweater with no sparkles or airplanes."

"When you try it on, come out and show us," said Nicole.

"You're not coming into the changing room with me?" squeaked Gumball.

"You're old enough to try on clothes by yourself now," his mother said.

"But . . ." Gumball's eyes got big, and his voice trailed off.

"But what?" asked Nicole.

"What if I get scared?" Gumball asked in a tiny voice.

"Very well," said Nicole. "Take Darwin with you."

"Hooray!" shouted Darwin, who grabbed Gumball's

hand, raced into the changing room, and slammed the door.

Anais and Nicole looked at each other, then down at the sweater that Nicole was still holding. Both of them sighed.

Anais knocked on the changing-room door. "Darwin? Gumball?"

"Aaaaaaaargh!" screamed Gumball.

"Go away!" shouted Darwin. "He's. Not. **DECENT!**"

"Well, he's going to stay that way unless you have this sweater for him to try on," Anais said.

Darwin's arm snaked out of the changing room and grabbed the sweater, then the door slammed closed again.

"Whew!" said Gumball. "That was close."

Darwin held out the hanger. "Your sweater, sir."

Gumball took the sweater off the hanger. He had to admit that it was nicer than his old one. There were no snags or holes. It smelled better, too. He buried his face in it and took a deep breath.

"What does it smell like?" asked Darwin.

"It smells . . . ," started Gumball.

"Yes?" asked Darwin.

". . . NEW."

Gumball and Darwin rubbed the sweater on their faces and took a deep breath of the new-sweater smell. Both of them got a little dizzy and fell backward onto the floor. From where they lay, they could see underneath the door of the changing room. Their eyes were very close to their mother's shoes. One of her feet was tapping. Impatiently.

“Boys?” she called. “Is everything okay?”

Gumball quickly jumped up, and Darwin began helping him into the sweater. “Yes, Mom!” they called through the door.

“Hurry up and come out here so I can see how the sweater fits.”

It took a few tries. **First Gumball got his head stuck in a sleeve.** Then his head and his arm were both through the neck hole. Then Darwin realized the whole thing was on backward.

“There’s something weird about this sweater,” said Darwin. “There’s just so much of it.”

“Yeah,” agreed Gumball. “It seems like there’s enough sweater here for both of us.”

Finally, Darwin opened the door of the changing room, and Gumball stepped out. Nicole had clearly chosen a sweater that was several sizes larger than the one he’d been wearing.

“Why is it so big?” Gumball asked.

“You’re growing as fast as bacteria in a trash can. I can’t buy you a new sweater every month,” said

Nicole. "You'll just have to grow into it. When you have your own money, you can buy as many sweaters as you like."

Gumball knew there was no use arguing with his mother, so he put on the too-large sweater and felt silly. Nicole was going to give his old one away, but Gumball knew that was no way to treat an old friend. "He deserves a proper good-bye," said Gumball.

"Fine," said Nicole.

The next morning, Nicole dropped Gumball, Darwin, and Anais off at school. Gumball took his old sweater to his locker. He was going to invite everyone to a ceremony in honor of his old sweater. He could even use it as an opportunity to talk to Penny. But when Gumball got to his locker, he couldn't open it.

"Why can't I open my locker?" Gumball said to himself. He tried and tried to spin the dial to get the right combination. "One," he said, when the dial reached the number one. "Three," he said, but the dial only made it to two.

"What's going on?" he asked Darwin. "Why can't I open my locker?"

"It's the sleeves!" Darwin said. It was true: The sleeves of the new sweater were so long, they went down past his hands. "The sweater is so big, it swallowed your hands!"

Gumball let his head fall against his locker with a *clank*. "This sweater is so big, I can't even open my locker!"

"Did you try pushing up the sleeves?" asked Darwin.

"That's not the point," Gumball grumbled. "Mom is ruining my life with this giant sweater. **I look like a shrimp.** I mean, how can I do homework if I can't even hold a pencil because the sleeves are too long? How am I supposed to go to gym when I can't catch a dodgeball? I'll just have to sit out until I grow into it."

Just at that moment, Penny came up to Gumball and Darwin.

"You look handsome today, Gumball," said Penny. "Did you get a new haircut?"

"No, Penny," said Gumball.

"Did you brush your teeth?" asked Penny.

"No," said Gumball. "I mean yes, I brushed my teeth, but that isn't what's new."

Darwin blurted out the news. "Our mom got Gumball this new sweater, and it's way too big. He can't even open his locker because the sleeves are so long."

"Hmmm," said Penny, looking closer. **"It is a bit on the large side."**

"I know!" said Gumball. "I tried to tell Mom it was too big, but she said I would have to grow into it."

"I think it makes you look handsome," said Penny. "And if you find a way to keep it from covering your hands, let me know. I'd like to hold one of them."

Penny walked away with a little wave. Luckily, Darwin was there to catch Gumball as he fell over.

"This is the WORST. THING. EVER!" shouted Gumball. "I look like a little tiny person lost in this gigantic sweater, and now Penny can't even hold hands with me!"

Suddenly, Darwin had an idea. “Gumball, you just need to grow into it faster!”

“Oh. Yeah,” said Gumball. “I guess. **But how do I grow faster?**”

“Let’s ask Mr. Dad,” said Darwin. “He’s really big, so he’ll probably know how to help you get bigger. And then you’ll fit into your sweater.”

“That’s a great idea, Darwin!” said Gumball. “You’re such a pal. Let’s ask him.”

The Smallest

Back at home, Gumball and Darwin found their dad sitting on the couch and watching TV, a bowl of sausages in his lap.

"Hey, Mr. Dad," said Darwin. "Gumball is embarrassed about his size. He wants to get bigger so he can fit in his sweater."

"Size isn't something to be embarrassed about, son," said Richard Watterson. "**But if you want, I can show you how to build muscle.** It's about time you started working out."

"That's great, Pop," said Gumball.

"The first step is lifting weights. So you'll need all the necessary equipment," explained Richard.

"Okay!" said Darwin. "What do we need?"

"Both of you go to the kitchen and fetch me a ham," said Richard. "One ham each."

"We need hams for lifting weights?" asked Gumball.

"Do you want to learn how to get bigger or not?" said Richard.

Gumball and Darwin ran off to the kitchen, and Richard got an old weight bench from the backyard shed. He dragged it around the house and set it up in the front yard.

"Do we have to do this in the front yard?" said Gumball, feeling embarrassed.

"The most important thing when lifting weights," said Richard, "is to make sure your friends and neighbors see you lifting weights. Now, did you get the hams like I asked?"

"Yes," they said, handing Richard two large hams from the refrigerator. **Richard stuck each ham on the end of the weight-lifting bar** and lay down on the bench.

"Why are we using hams?" said Gumball.

"I lost the weights in a boating accident," said Richard. "Also, it's important to have protein after a workout. This way we can lift weights and then get our post-workout protein right away!"

Richard made a loud grunting sound and lifted the bar with the hams on each end over his head. He lowered it to his chest. Ham juice ran down the bar from both ends, meeting in the middle, and dripped

into Richard's open mouth. The ham was too delicious for Richard to resist. With one push, he flung the bar straight up and sucked the ham off each end like it was a lollipop. "That's enough for today," said Richard.

"But I didn't get to do it. How am I supposed to get big enough to fit in my sweater?" Gumball asked, looking at the greasy ham bar.

"I suppose you'll just have to grow into it, son," said Richard, wiping the ham juice off his mouth.

Just then a deep rumbling sound interrupted them. A large bus came to a stop right in front of their house. It was an open-top double-decker bus, and every seat was filled with a tourist peering down at the Wattersons. Across the side of the bus were painted words: *The Tour of Elmore.*

"On your right you'll see the Wattersons' house," said the tour-bus driver over a loudspeaker. "This is **THE SMALLEST HOUSE IN ELMORE**." The driver's voice was so loud coming through the speaker that it seemed to shake the entire neighborhood.

Every tourist *ooh*ed and *aah*ed at the sight of the smallest house in Elmore. Some even snapped photos with their cameras and phones. Then the bus drove away as fast as it had appeared.

"What was that?" asked Darwin.

"I think that tour-bus driver just said we live in the smallest house in all of Elmore," said Gumball.

"WAAAAA!" Richard burst into tears and ran into the house.

"We can't live in the smallest house in Elmore," said Gumball. He and Darwin turned around to look at their house.

"It *is* pretty small," said Darwin.

"Yeah, but the smallest?" said Gumball. "**How can it be the smallest?** What about the house on the corner? The yellow one."

"That's a fire hydrant," said Darwin.

"Oh," said Gumball.

Gumball and Darwin went into the house. Nicole was in the kitchen, writing a list of chores on the refrigerator.

"Mom," said Gumball, "do we really live in the smallest house in Elmore?"

Nicole sighed. **"There's nothing wrong with our house, Gumball,"** she said.

"But Dad just cried when a tour bus drove by and the driver said that our house—"

Nicole interrupted Gumball. "There's nothing wrong with our house!" she said. She was suddenly very angry, and grabbed her purse and keys from the counter. "I'm going to work. Don't talk about the size of the house again. Especially not to your father."

Nicole slammed the front door on her way out. Gumball and Darwin stared after her, very surprised by her behavior.

"Something's not right," said Gumball.

"I'll say," said Darwin, looking at the chore chart. "She gave you the vacuuming. She always gives me the vacuuming because I love it."

"No, Darwin," said Gumball. "If there was nothing wrong with our house, why would Mom act like that? There is something very suspicious about the house." He paused for a moment to think.

"We need to find out about the house," Gumball decided.

"Okay," said Darwin.

Gumball and Darwin walked into the living room.

"We need to confirm that the house is the smallest in Elmore," said Gumball.

"How do we do that?" asked Darwin.

"Well, I mean, look at this place," said Gumball, as he swept his arms out in front of him. **"You can't even swing a cat in here."**

"Really?" asked Darwin. He grabbed Gumball by the tail and swung him around in a circle. Gumball's head smashed into a lamp on the nearby table, and the whole thing went crashing to the floor. Then Gumball slammed into a picture on the wall with a **CRASH** before Darwin dropped him onto the floor.

"Dude!" said Gumball, grabbing his head. "Why'd you do that?"

"You told me to," said Darwin. "You said to swing a cat! And you were right: There's not enough room."

"It was a figure of speech, buddy."

"Oh. I'm sorry."

"It's okay," said Gumball. "I know what else we can do—let's see how long it takes us to run from one end of the house to the other!"

"That'll be less dangerous, I guess," said Darwin.

CHAPTER THREE

The Hat

Gumball and Darwin went up to their room, and Darwin pulled out a stopwatch. Anais happened to walk by the room at that moment, and saw Darwin with Gumball crouched in a starting position.

"What are you guys doing?" she asked.

“Timing how long it takes to run through the house,” said Darwin.

“Are you sure that’s a good idea?” said Anais.

“How else are we going to make sure that our house is the smallest in Elmore?” said Gumball.

“There’s a reason Mom says not to run through the house,” said Anais. “It’s dangerous, and you could crash into something and get hurt—”

“GO!” shouted Darwin, ignoring Anais.

Gumball dashed out the door, almost knocking over his sister. He turned the corner at the top of the stairs and raced down them, taking two at a time.

“See?” shouted Gumball. “There’s nothing to it!”

The moment these words left his lips, **Gumball’s feet slipped on the stairs,** and he sailed into the air. He bounced down the rest of the stairs and slammed into the floor by the front door.

“Owww!” he groaned, but wasted no time picking himself up and dashing toward the kitchen, but as he raced through the living room, he tripped on the rug and flew through the kitchen doorway, crashing into the cabinets!

“Yowch!” he cried. This time picking himself up wasn’t very easy. He continued toward the back door. Even though he wasn’t moving quite as fast, he

reached the back door sooner than he anticipated, and smacked into that, too.

"Aargh . . . ," moaned Gumball as he opened the door that led into the backyard.

"Thirty seconds!" announced Darwin cheerfully from the bedroom window above. Gumball collapsed on the ground, trying to catch his breath.

"See?" said Gumball, panting as he pulled himself back upstairs. "I bet it takes at least a whole minute to run through Banana Joe's house, and his house is pretty small, too. **Our house must be half the size of a normal house.** This proves it!"

"You're so smart," said Darwin.

Anais rolled her eyes. "Our house may be the smallest, but running through it in thirty seconds doesn't prove anything, except maybe that you aren't very coordinated."

Gumball ignored this comment. "What we need to figure out next is *why* the Watterson house is the smallest," he said.

"Agreed," said Darwin. "There have to be clues around here somewhere."

"Hmmm," said Gumball, stroking his chin. "Where should we look?"

"How about the attic?" said Darwin. "We've

discovered lots of other secrets in the attic!"

"Of course!" said Gumball. "What would I do without you, Darwin?"

"Probably not run through the house when you're not supposed to," said Anais.

"No, I'd probably still do that," said Gumball.

Anais followed as Gumball and Darwin ran back upstairs. At the end of the hallway there was a little door in the ceiling that hid a ladder leading up to the attic.

"Give me a boost!" Gumball told Darwin.

"Give me a break!" said Anais, shaking her head. "I'm not going to watch you two hurt yourselves again. I'm going to go play with Daisy." She turned and headed toward her room.

Darwin got down on all fours, and Gumball took a running start, then catapulted off Darwin's back. As he flew toward the ceiling, Gumball grabbed the little cord that pulled open the attic door. The door swung down, and the ladder unfolded with a loud **CLANK**, and a long **SQUEEEEEEEAK**.

"That was awesome," said Darwin.

"Thanks for the assist," said Gumball.

They climbed up into the stuffy dark space above. The attic was quiet and dusty, as always, stacked with boxes and lots of other things that the Wattersons had forgotten were even there.

As their eyes adjusted to the dim light, **Darwin noticed something else about the attic**.

"It's very quiet up here," he said.

"Yeah," said Gumball. "Almost too quiet."

"Maybe secrets like the quiet best," said Darwin.

"Keeping quiet is the *point* of secrets," said a voice behind them. Gumball and Darwin

just about jumped out of their skins.

"WHO'S THERE?" shouted Gumball.

Anais flipped on a flashlight. “It’s just me, scaredy-cat.”

Darwin started giggling. “I thought you weren’t coming up here,” he said.

Anais shrugged. “I got curious,” she said. “Plus, I figured you two would have a better chance of finding a clue if I brought you a flashlight.”

“There’s a million secret things we can find up here,” said Gumball. He and Darwin began rooting through boxes, throwing things aside that didn’t seem to be clues.

“Maybe one of them will be what we’re looking for,” said Darwin.

“Remind me again what you’re doing,” said Anais.

“We’re looking for something that will tell us why our house is the smallest one in Elmore,” said Gumball.

“What could you possibly find up here that would explain that?” asked Anais.

“I dunno,” said Gumball. “But I’ll know it when I see it.”

“Is this it?” asked Darwin, holding up a fishing pole.

“Nope,” said Gumball.

“What about this?” asked Darwin. **He was holding a purple feather boa** that he wrapped around his neck.

“Focus, buddy,” said Gumball. “We’re looking for clues about the size of our house.”

“Oh, right,” said Darwin.

Anais sighed. “I think it might just be that big houses cost more money. Maybe this house was all

Mom and Dad could afford."

Gumball began to laugh. "Anais, don't be ridiculous. Why would we live in the smallest house in Elmore if it wasn't for some big, secret reason?"

"Not having enough money is a good reason," said Anais.

"Everyone knows that if you don't have enough money, you just go to the bank," said Gumball.

"Ugh," said Anais. "That's not how it works."

"Wait!" shouted Gumball, pointing to something Darwin had uncovered. "What's that?"

Darwin pulled on it, and out popped an oversize teddy bear.

"That's a clue!" said Gumball. "**We're really on to something.** Keep looking!"

"How is THAT a clue?" asked Anais.

Gumball didn't answer her. Instead he dived back into the boxes and began searching for other clues.

"This doesn't make any sense," said Anais.

Darwin was cuddling up with the huge, fluffy teddy bear. "This is all I really need to be happy," he said.

"Darwin!" shouted Gumball. "What are you doing?"

"Sorry!" said Darwin. "It's just so cuddly, I couldn't resist."

"We have to find more clues!" said Gumball. He

dug through more boxes. “Ah-HA!” he said as he held up a gigantic foam cowboy hat.

“A big foam cowboy hat?” said Anais. “How is that a clue about the size of our house?”

“Don’t you see?” asked Gumball. “It all makes sense.”

“Does it?” asked Anais.

“The **GIANT** teddy bear,” said Gumball, “and the **GIANT** hat! Our house isn’t actually small.”

“It’s not?” asked Darwin.

“No!” said Gumball. “It only feels small because we are **GIANTS, TOO!**”

“WHAT?!” said Anais. “That’s ridiculous.”

“Why else would we have giant things? Think about it. If we were small, the house would seem huge. Instead, the house seems small, so *we* must be *huge*, and these things prove it!”

“That’s just some of Dad’s old stuff from college,” said Anais, pointing to the logo on the giant hat. “See? It says *Elmore U.* And that teddy bear came from a carnival game. Dad won it for Mom when they were dating. Those things are supposed to be giant to make them funny.”

“You can deny it all you want, Anais,” said Gumball. “We are a family of **GIANTS**.”

"Whatever," said Anais. "Enjoy being a giant!"

Gumball and Darwin watched Anais climb down the ladder and disappear from the attic.

"She's just jealous," said Gumball.

"Are you sure, dude?" said Darwin. "Can you really be a giant? Think of how perfectly you fit into your bed."

"Darwin—please," said Gumball. "Think about it. Why else would the house feel small? Being a giant is the only explanation."

"Is it?" said Darwin.

"Just let me enjoy this," said Gumball.

"Fine," said Darwin. "But I'm happy with my size. You can be a giant."

Darwin went down the attic ladder, leaving Gumball by himself.

"I will!" shouted Gumball. "I mean, I AM!"

Gumball put on the giant hat and picked up the giant teddy bear. He began to stomp around the attic. In a giant-size voice, he started to chant: **"FE-FI-FO-FUM! I AM A GIANT WATTERSON."** But just as he stomped by the opening in the floor where the ladder led back down to the hallway, the giant foam cowboy hat fell over his eyes, and he stepped into the hole.

The noise of Gumball falling out of the attic

brought Darwin and Anais running into the hall from their bedrooms. They found Gumball on top of the big teddy bear, his face covered by the oversize cowboy hat. Luckily, all the foam and teddy-bear stuffing had broken his fall.

"Are you okay?" asked Darwin.

"When will you believe me that you aren't a giant?" asked Anais.

"Of course I'm a giant," said Gumball, dusting himself off. "That was a giant fall."

CHAPTER FOUR

The Shrimp

The next day at school, Darwin was sitting at a lunch table with Alan and Masami. "We live in the smallest house in Elmore," he told them.

"Yeah, we know," said Masami.

"You do?"

"Yes, everyone knows the Wattersons live in the smallest house in Elmore," said Alan. "It's even on the tour."

"Oh," said Darwin. "How does everybody know about that tour?"

Before Alan or Masami could answer, **the ground began to shake**.

"What's that?" asked Alan.

"It's an earthquake!" said Masami.

"No," said Darwin. "It's just Gumball. He thinks he's a giant."

Gumball stomped up behind them. He was

walking funny, like his legs were too big to move, hunched over as if his head might hit the ceiling. He was shaking the floor as hard as he could with every step.

"HEY, GUYS," Gumball said in a very low, very loud voice. **"FE-FI-FO-FUM! I AM A GIANT WATTERSON."**

Masami laughed. “Gumball, what are you doing?”

“Just being my giant self,” he said. “We Wattersons come from a long line of giants!”

“You’re not a giant,” said Masami.

“Of course I am,” said Gumball. “It’s why our house seems so small. It’s not that the house is so little; it’s that the Wattersons are so BIG.”

“You just live in a tiny house,” said Alan. “Even Banana Joe’s house is bigger than yours.”

“That’s exactly what a jealous non-giant would say,” said Gumball, trying not to let Masami and Alan get to him.

“You’re not a giant,” said Darwin. “If you were a giant, you’d be as big as Hector.”

“I am too a giant!” said Gumball. “See how much bigger I am than Alan? He used to be taller than me, and now I’m taller than him.”

“That’s because Alan is sitting on the bench

instead of floating in the air like he usually does," said Darwin.

"I'll prove I'm a giant!" said Gumball.

"This I'd like to see," said Masami.

Gumball looked around the lunchroom, desperate to prove that he was big.

"I'll—I'll—" he stuttered. Suddenly he saw a way he could prove that he was big. "I'll pick a fight with Tina!"

The lunchroom suddenly fell silent, and Gumball immediately regretted what he'd said.

"That's not a good idea," said Darwin.

In his head, Gumball agreed, and though he could have said he was just joking and taken it back, he was too proud to do that. "If that's what it takes to convince you guys," said Gumball, "then it's the only way."

"No, it's not, dude," said Darwin. "Don't pick a fight with Tina."

"You leave me no choice. My honor is at stake," said Gumball.

Darwin sighed, knowing Gumball was going to do what he wanted to do, even if they both knew it was a bad idea.

"Okay," said Darwin.

Gumball approached Tina, who was standing in line to get some Salisbury steak from the lunch lady.

"Hey, Tina," said Gumball. "Or should I say, 'Hey, **TINY!**'"

Tina's eyes narrowed, and she swung her huge head around to glare at Gumball. Her teeth separated and a massive glob of drool ran down her chin and landed with a *plop!* on Gumball's head. "What did you call me?" she growled.

Gumball was terrified. His knees were shaking and he couldn't speak. He suddenly realized that the only thing giant about him was the error he'd just made.

"Um, I was just saying 'Hi, Tina,' but I must have jumbled the words together and it sounded like I called you Tiny," said Gumball, trying to cover up his mistake. Tina couldn't be fooled. She narrowed her eyes, lifted her gigantic foot, and stepped on him.

"So do you still think you're a giant?" asked Darwin, helping Gumball up from the lunchroom floor.

"No," said Gumball, his head hanging low. "I guess I'm more of a shrimp."

"You're not a shrimp," said Darwin. "You just haven't grown up yet."

"I don't know," said Gumball. "Everything around me seems either too big or too small."

"**You're the perfect size for who you are**, and I wouldn't want you to be any different."

Gumball smiled. "Thanks, buddy. You really know how to make things better."

"Anytime," said Darwin.

"But we still haven't figured out why we live in the smallest house in Elmore!" said Gumball.

"Oh," said Darwin, his face falling. "We're still doing that?"

"Yes!" shouted Gumball.

The Guilt

The Wattersons were seated around the table having microwaved TV dinners. Nicole noticed that Gumball was twirling his fork around in his food, looking glum. "Gumball," she said, "what's the matter?"

Gumball made his voice sound higher and softer than usual. He was trying to make his mother feel sorry for him. "I thought we were a family of giants," he said.

"He picked a fight with Tina today," said Darwin.

"You did what?" asked Nicole.

"I just wanted to prove I was as big as her," said Gumball. "But I'm a shrimp who can't even fit into my sweater. I won't ever amount to anything because I'm not big enough."

"I was small once," said Richard, "and now look at me. All grown up and a success."

"Richard," said Nicole, "you may have been younger, but you were never small. Gumball, lots of good things are small. Birds are small, and they make beautiful music. Pennies are small, and they bring good luck. Even TV dinners are small, but look how much fun they are to eat!"

At that moment, everyone's stomach growled because the meals were too small.

Nicole laughed nervously. "The point is, lots of things come in small sizes, but it doesn't limit their potential, and you have so much potential, Gumball."

"Thanks, Mom," Gumball said. He went back to twirling his food. "Maybe someday I'll reach it."

Later that night, when they went to bed, Darwin thought he saw Gumball smile.

"I'm glad you've found a way to be happy about the size of the house," said Darwin. "That's very mature of you."

"I'm not happy about that," said Gumball. "I'm

happy because I set in motion my most brilliant plan yet."

"You did?" said Darwin. "I didn't notice."

"Yes," said Gumball. "At dinner when I pretended to be sad about my size, I was really just trying to make Mom feel sorry for me."

"You were pretending?" asked Darwin.

"Yes," Gumball said. "Even now, Mom is in her bed, tossing and turning, guilt tearing at her from the inside, eating at her conscience like a starving animal."

"Oh, I don't like starving animals," said Darwin.

"It's only a matter of time before she breaks down," continued Gumball. "She won't be able to handle it. By tomorrow night she will crack and tell me why our house is the smallest one in Elmore." Gumball gave a loud, evil laugh.

"I'm trying to go to sleep!" shouted Anais from her bedroom.

"Sorry!" said Gumball.

"I don't know," said Darwin. "**Mom is a total pro at guilt trips.** I think she's immune to them."

"Maybe to yours," said Gumball. "Just you wait. She'll tell. Oh, she'll tell." Gumball rolled over in his bed, laughing to himself.

Darwin shrugged and turned out the light.

As he slept, Gumball dreamed he was standing in a large, beautiful ballroom. "Where am I?" he asked. The ballroom was so big, his voice echoed off the walls far and wide. "Where is everyone?"

Gumball ran around the ballroom. "It's so big!" he shouted, laughing and jumping for joy. "**There's so much room for me to reach my potential!** I can even run around as fast as I want. I must tell Darwin. Darwin!"

Gumball ran across the ballroom to the doorway, searching for Darwin. But the room was so large, and the door was so far away, that it took him a very long time to reach it. By the time he did, Gumball was out of breath.

The door was so big and heavy that he almost couldn't open it. "Darwin?" called Gumball. Beyond the gigantic ballroom was a long hall. "Oh man, this place is too big. Darwin? Where are you?"

There was no answer, so Gumball took off down the long hallway. He passed window after window as he ran. It seemed like the hallway would never end. By the time Gumball reached the end of it, he was tired and out of breath again. He opened the next heavy door.

"Darwin!" he shouted. "Where are you?"

But there was no answer. Just beyond the door was a very long staircase that descended to the floor below. "I'm gonna be a track star when I get to the end of this place," panted Gumball as he took the stairs two at a time.

The stairs didn't seem to end. "Mom!" he shouted. "Darwin! Anais! Dad!" But there was no answer. "Where is everyone?" he said. "To have such a huge house and no one to share it with!"

Gumball awoke with a start.

"Dude, what's wrong?" asked Darwin.

"I had the worst dream," said Gumball. "I dreamed I was alone in a great big mansion that went on forever and ever."

"Wow! Did you run around as fast as you wanted?" Darwin asked.

"I could have. But that's not the point," said Gumball. "I couldn't find anyone."

"Maybe it's a sign that you shouldn't be so concerned about the size of our house?" said Darwin.

Gumball thought about it for a moment. "Nah," he said. "I think it means that a big mansion is my dream house."

In the morning, Gumball and Darwin went downstairs for breakfast. As they were eating cereal, Nicole came downstairs, and Gumball nudged Darwin. "Watch and learn," he said. Then he put on a big smile and said, "Oh! Good morning, Mom!"

"Good morning, sweethearts," said Nicole. She was dressed and ready for work.

"I couldn't sleep," said Gumball. "I had a horrible dream that I lived in a big empty mansion all by myself. I'm sorry I tried to make you feel bad about the size of our house yesterday!"

"Oh, that's all right, Gumball," said Nicole. "I slept like a baby."

"Rats!" said Gumball.

"You boys have a wonderful day at school." Nicole kissed each of them on the forehead and left for work.

"Oh man," said Gumball.

"I told you it wouldn't work," said Darwin.

"I know she's hiding something!" shouted Gumball. "I know there's a reason why our house is the smallest one in Elmore."

Gumball hadn't noticed Richard. He had come downstairs, and was standing in the doorway of the kitchen when Gumball said this. When Richard heard

what Gumball said, he started crying. Then he turned around and went running back upstairs.

"Oh no," said Gumball.

"I think he picked up the phone," said Darwin.

Sure enough, Gumball and Darwin heard their father's muffled voice saying something about Gumball. A moment later the front door burst open. It was Nicole. Her face was red with anger.

"Gumball Watterson! I told you not to bring up the size of our house again! Go to your room!"

"But what about school?" asked Gumball.

Nicole was so mad, she had forgotten about school. "**Go to school!** Then go right to your room when you get home!"

Nicole slammed the door and left for work again.

"Wow. Mom was really mad," said Darwin.

"I'm going to find out what they're hiding," grumbled Gumball, "even if it means I have to stay in my room for the rest of my life. Nobody acts that suspicious unless they have something to hide."

"I have to agree with you," said Anais. "Maybe there really *is* a secret reason the house is so small."

"Of course there is!" said Gumball. **"What would the Wattersons be without secrets?"**

CHAPTER SIX

The Plans

After school, Gumball was pacing his room. He was growing restless. Anais and Darwin were sitting on the bed, watching him wear a track in the carpet.

"There's got to be a way to find out why our

house is the smallest in Elmore," he told them. "Maybe we could disappear and **make it look like a kidnapping**, and for a ransom we could demand to know why the house is so small."

"Maybe," said Darwin. "But you've been talking about this for days now."

"Yeah," said Anais. "Do you really think Mom will be fooled by kidnappers asking why the house is so small, instead of asking for money?"

"You're right," said Gumball. "That won't work. We need **something more diabolical**."

"Why don't you just go to the city planning office and ask for the house plans?" said Anais.

"That's it!" said Gumball. "Of course! The city is the reason our house is so small. The oppressive government doesn't want us to live in a big house. We must go down to City Hall and fight for our right to live large!"

Anais sighed. "Sometimes I think I'm speaking a different language." She got up and left Gumball and Darwin to their plans.

They opened their bedroom window and slid down the drainpipe. Then they crawled across the backyard on their elbows and knees like soldiers in combat. When they reached the back fence, Gumball boosted Darwin over, then scrambled over himself. **They took off running for Elmore City Hall,** where the city planning offices were located. "I bet our house was supposed to be four—no, *five* times as big as it is," said Gumball. "With six floors and an indoor theater."

"I bet it was supposed to have a roller-skating rink!" said Darwin.

"Of course!" said Gumball. "And an indoor pool!"

"And a rare-bird aviary!" shouted Darwin.

When Gumball and Darwin finally reached the city planning offices, they found a receptionist sitting at the information desk. She looked like a nice old lady.

"Hello," said Gumball. "We'd like the building plans for the Watterson house."

"Oh, you mean the smallest house in Elmore?" said the receptionist. She didn't look so nice to Gumball anymore. Now she seemed kind of crotchety.

"What?" said Gumball. **"Just give us the plans!"**

"Only adults can sign for plans," said the receptionist. "Are you an adult?"

"No," said Gumball.

She turned to Darwin. "And are *you* an adult?"

"No," said Darwin.

"Then I can't give you the plans."

"Jeez!" said Gumball. He grabbed Darwin's hand and marched out in a huff.

"I guess we'll never get the house plans," said Darwin. "Good-bye, rare-bird aviary."

"Oh, Darwin," said Gumball, "now's not the time to give up!"

"What do you mean?" asked Darwin. "She said no."

"Are you going to let city hall take away your lifelong dream of a rare-bird aviary?" said Gumball.

"Do you have an idea for another way to get the plans?" asked Darwin hopefully.

Gumball sighed. “Oh, Darwin. Have we just met?”

Before Darwin could answer, Gumball grabbed his hand and dragged him down the hall.

A few minutes later, a tall figure walked back down the hall. He was wearing a long trench coat and a fedora pulled low over his eyes, and he sported a funny-looking mustache.

The man marched right up to the receptionist. She thought there was something strange about him, but she couldn’t quite figure out what it was. He walked like he was dizzy, and his mustache looked like a mop, but this was Elmore after all, so she just said, “How may I help you?”

“Hi,” said Gumball in as low a voice as he could muster. “We would like the plans to the Watterson house.”

“The smallest—” started the receptionist.

“Yes! **The smallest house in Elmore!**” said Gumball impatiently.

“That’s the second time today someone has asked for the plans to the Watterson house,” said the receptionist. “There must be something really special about it.”

“Yes!” cried Gumball, snatching the plans from the receptionist. He jumped off Darwin, out of the trench coat, and bolted for the door.

CITY PLANNING

"Hey!" shouted the receptionist. "You're the same kids who asked the first time!"

"Thank you," Darwin shouted over his shoulder. He didn't want to be impolite, but he wasn't going to stick around and see what happened.

"Are you ready for this?" said Gumball after they reached home.

"Yes! Yes!" Darwin shouted, jumping up and down.

"I don't know, bro," said Gumball. "What we find in here could be totally shocking. It—"

"Just open them!" shouted Darwin. Gumball smiled and unrolled the plans.

"OH. MY. GOSH," said Gumball.

"What?" asked Darwin.

Gumball's face began to turn red, and he balled up his fists in anger.

"What? What?" cried Darwin. "What's wrong with them?"

"Nothing!" shouted Gumball. "There's nothing wrong with them! The house is exactly how it's drawn here."

"Let me see!" said Darwin, snatching the plans away. "You're right!" he said. "There's nothing wrong. The house was supposed to be just like this all along!"

"Where's the indoor pool?" demanded Gumball. "Where's the indoor theater? The roller-skating rink?"

"Don't forget the rare-bird aviary," said Darwin.

"I don't get it, Darwin," said Gumball. "Anais was right. This is all the house Mom and Dad could afford. **There's no conspiracy after all.** And I'm not giant. Our house is just small."

"Cheer up," said Darwin. "At least we don't live in the yellow house on the corner."

Darwin smiled at his joke, but it didn't cheer Gumball up at all.

The Inch

Anais came out of the house.

"Did you find anything wrong with the plans?" she asked.

"No," said Gumball and Darwin gloomily.

"Maybe it's **okay that we live in the smallest house** in Elmore," said Anais. "Think about it. How long does it take you to get a snack in the middle of the night when you're hungry?"

"Not very long," said Gumball.

"In a bigger house, it'd take twice as long!" said Darwin.

"Also, vacuuming and chores would take so much longer!" said Anais.

"Yeah," said Gumball, starting to feel better. "We don't have to spend as much time doing chores!"

"Exactly!" exclaimed Anais. "That's the spirit."

"And because the house is so small, Mom and

Dad can't have any more kids," said Gumball. "There'd be nowhere to put them. If we had a dozen other brothers and sisters in a bigger house, I wouldn't be as spoiled."

"I'm not sure that's a good thing," said Anais, "but, yeah. **Way to look at the bright side!**"

"Yeah, I guess it's okay that we live in a smaller house. Still, sometimes I wish we had an indoor pool."

"You can swim in my fishbowl if it helps you feel better," said Darwin.

"Thanks, buddy," said Gumball. "You're the best friend a guy could want."

Gumball rolled up the house plans. "Let's give these back to the city," he said. Disappointed that they had not discovered a conspiracy about why the Watterson house was so small, Gumball and Darwin headed back to City Hall.

"Wait!" Anais shouted. "I've just realized something."

She ran into the house and came back out waiving a ruler.

"What is it?" asked Gumball.

"There *is* something wrong with them!" said Anais.

"I knew it! There's a conspiracy!" shouted Gumball. He frantically unrolled the plans.

"Here," said Anais, pointing to the marks at the bottom of the pages. "This mark indicates the scale of the plans. See how it says one inch equals one foot?"

"Uh-huh," said Gumball and Darwin, but Anais could tell they didn't really know what she was talking about.

"It means that one inch on this piece of paper equals one foot in the real world. Architects call this drawing a plan 'to scale.' That way they don't have to draw a plan the actual size of the house, which wouldn't fit on a piece of paper. The builder reads the scale of the plan and then buys the materials at the actual size indicated by the scale. That way the house can be built the right size."

"So?" said Gumball.

"So!" said Anais. "Look at this!" She held the ruler against the scale at the bottom of the paper. One inch on the ruler was twice as big as one inch on the scale.

"It's too small!" shouted Gumball. "Someone made the house small on purpose!"

"Exactly," said Anais. "By half."

"We won!" shouted Gumball. "We finally found out the truth!"

"Not quite," said Anais. "Someone knows something they're not telling. Why are the plans so small? Why didn't it get fixed?"

"Maybe the plans got put in the washer and dryer?" said Darwin.

"That's ridiculous," said Gumball. "You can't wash house plans. **No, someone did this on purpose.**"

"Why would someone do it on purpose?" said Darwin.

"Maybe to cheat Mom and Dad out of a big house!" said Gumball.

"The builder could have done it," said Anais. "He probably charged Mom and Dad for a full-size house and then only built them a half-size one."

"We have to tell them," said Gumball.

“But if we bring it up again, she’ll ground you!” said Darwin.

“It’s a risk I’m willing to take. We’ve got to make it right! Don’t you want an indoor theater? Don’t you want an indoor skating rink?”

“And a rare-bird aviary!” shouted Darwin.

“Finally,” said Gumball. **"We will know the truth about our tiny house!"**

The Biggest

As the Wattersons sat down to a delicious meal, Gumball's fork and knife chattered on the plate.

"Gumball, honey," said Nicole, "what in the world is going on?"

"Oh, nothing," he said. "I just thought I'd make you some dessert tonight."

"That's so sweet of you," said Nicole. "What are we going to have?"

"HUMBLE PIE!" he shouted. Gumball pulled out the house plans and slammed them down on the table. Nicole's face was full of surprise, then anger.

"I told you not to bring this up ever again!" she yelled.

Gumball interrupted. "We know the house is half the size it's supposed to be!"

"What are you talking about?" asked Nicole with a

nervous, fake smile. "It is not."

"It's true," said Anais. "Someone changed the scale of the house plans." She took out her ruler and placed it against the plans' scale. "See?"

At that moment, Gumball, Darwin, and Anais didn't notice how much **Richard was fidgeting in his seat**, but Nicole did.

"It's no one's fault the house is built the way it is," said Nicole. "Sometimes things just happen. Now I want you to stop talking about this and eat your dinner!"

"WAAAA!" Richard suddenly burst into tears. Gumball, Darwin, and Anais were all very surprised.

"Richard, what's wrong?" asked Nicole.

"It's all my fault!" he shouted. "I'm the reason the house is so small!"

"What are you talking about?" said Gumball. "Why would you build the house too small?"

"I didn't mean to," said Richard to the kids. "It was years ago, when Gumball was just a little guy. Your mother and I had finally saved enough money to buy a house. I was up late one night, working hard to

make sure the house was just right. I tried to make it perfect in every way."

Then Richard turned to Nicole. "The next morning," he said, "I woke up on the plans. I had fallen asleep, and my banana split had melted all over the blueprints. **There was chocolate sauce and melted ice cream everywhere.** I was so worried you'd get mad at me that I rushed to the Laundromat and put them in the wash. When I pulled them out of the dryer, I was so excited that they were clean again that I didn't notice they had shrunk, and I continued building. I'm sorry. It's all my fault we live in the smallest house in Elmore." Richard hung his head and began to sob.

"I knew it!" shouted Gumball. "There was a conspiracy! I knew it, I knew it, I knew it."

"Gumball, stop it!" said Nicole. Gumball sat down in his chair.

Nicole smiled at Richard. "Oh, honey," she said. "I knew the whole time that you'd accidentally shrunk the plans."

"You did?" Richard sounded very surprised, sniffling.

"Yes. When I went to work that morning years and years ago, I left you sleeping on the plans. You looked so comfortable snoring on the blueprints that I didn't want to wake you. Later, when the plans were clean, I saw they'd shrunk. I didn't want you to feel bad, so I didn't say anything."

"Really?" said Richard. "So all these years, I've been feeling guilty and I didn't need to?"

"Yes," said Nicole. "I forgive you."

"Thank you, sweetheart," said Richard with a smile.

"You mean there was no diabolical plot to make our house the smallest in Elmore?" asked Gumball. "After all we went through, it turns out that Dad just put the plans through the wash, and you let it happen? What a rip-off! **And now we still have to live in the smallest house in Elmore.** I want an indoor theater! I want a roller-skating rink!"

"What about my rare-bird aviary?" asked Darwin.

"It's okay, Gumball," said Nicole. "We can't afford a bigger house, or all those indoor attractions. Our house may be small, but you know what?"

"What?" said Gumball.

"I love our house."

"You do?" said Gumball, not understanding.

"Yes," said Nicole. "I love it because it's cozy and comfortable. It stays warm and it's easy to clean.

But most of all, I love it because living in a small house means the people I love most in my life are never very far away."

"Oh," said Gumball. "I never thought of it that way."

"I love you kids, and you, Richard," said Nicole. "If we lived in a big house and you all had your own rooms, we might not be as close as we are here. In a small house, we don't have to worry about that at all. We're always close."

"*Awww*, I love our house, too," said Richard with a sniffle.

"I love you, Mom and Dad," said Gumball. "I guess you're right. No one else can say they live in the smallest house in Elmore!"

DRIVE-THRU

"I love our house, too," said Anais.

"So do I," said Darwin. "But it could still use a rare-bird aviary."

The Wattersons all laughed and finished their dinner. For dessert, instead of the humble pie Gumball had planned, Nicole served a different kind of pie. These were tiny pies she had picked up from the grocery store on the way home from work. Each one was just enough for a single person. Every bite was delicious, but **Gumball loved it most because it was just the right size**.

THE END

AND NOW. . . AN EXCERPT FROM:

The Amazing World of Gumball

Once Upon a Time in Elmore

When Gumball Met Penny

By Wrigley Stuart

CHAPTER ONE

The Cheese Head

The neon numbers on the alarm clock flashed from 1:59 a.m. to 2:00 a.m. Yet Gumball Watterson lay on his bedcovers, eyes open. This was no time for a nine-year-old to be wide awake. He stared at the wooden slats of the top bunk above him. No one slept up there. Instead, the sound of snoring came from Darwin's fishbowl.

School started in the morning. Gumball's mind filled with a combination of excitement and dread. He was excited to see his friends again, but incredibly bummed that summer vacation was over.

Gumball stared at his clock.

The numbers now read 2:01.

Would morning never come?

Gumball got out of bed, tiptoed into the hallway, and then headed down the stairs.

If he couldn't sleep, then Gumball might as well

do something important, like watch TV.

Gumball yawned as he sat on the living room couch. He dug in between the seat cushions, pulling out the television remote control. He flipped through channels of **boring infomercials and reruns**. Cartoons weren't on this late. Or was it *this early*? Gumball was too groggy to think straight, but too antsy to sleep. He breathed deeply, his eyelids feeling heavy, and he watched a show about a blender.

It was an awesome blender. Not only did the machine cut, chip, whip, and puree fruits and veggies, but it could also cut, chip, whip, and puree watches, a digital camera, and a key chain. Gumball eyed the phone number flashing at the bottom of the screen. If he ordered the blender within the next thirty seconds, he would also get a set of knives.

He imagined blending his sneakers, a lightbulb, and the bowl of Cheezy-Bites snacks that sat on the coffee table in front of him.

His dad must have left the bowl out last night.

Gumball's mind floated off, dreaming of various electronics mangled and mixed from high-performance blending. His eyelids once again grew heavy, his breathing slowed, and he drifted off to sleep.

"Wake up!"

Gumball's eyes popped open, and he saw a sea of orange.

He had fallen asleep with his head in the bowl of Cheezy-Bites.

Gumball's mother stood over him. Nicole Watterson was dressed for work in her Rainbow Factory uniform: a gray skirt, a white shirt, and, of course, her rainbow-colored badge. "You'll be late for school!"

Gumball's father, Richard Watterson, stood next to her. He adjusted his black work tie and patted the red woolen cap he always wore on his head. He rubbed a finger across Gumball's forehead. "Yum! Processed cheese dust!" he exclaimed as he licked his finger.

"Hurry! School!" Mrs. Watterson shouted.

Gumball bolted off the sofa and into the bathroom. He stared in the mirror. He gasped. The top half of his light-blue head was coated with Cheezy-Bites cheese powder. He wiped his forehead as hard as he could with a hand towel.

The orange stain refused to budge.

"My head is orange!" squealed a panicked Gumball.

Darwin stood in the bathroom doorway. "What's wrong with having an orange head?" he asked.

"Sure, orange looks good on *you*," cried Gumball. "But I can't go to school like this!"

"You'll have to," said Darwin. "There's no time to wash it off. Mrs. Mom says we have to hurry or we're going to miss the bus."

Gumball squeezed between Darwin and the door frame and dashed to the hall closet. "No . . . no . . . maybe," he mumbled, as he rummaged through a large cardboard box at the back of the closet.

"Why are you looking at our old Halloween costumes?" asked Darwin.

Gumball grabbed a pirate hat, glared at it, and then threw it back into the box. A moment later, Gumball emerged from the closet. **A large black fedora** with a small white feather was perched on his head.

"Why are you dressed like a 1920s gangster?" asked Darwin.

"Because I look awesome!" Gumball announced. He puffed out his chest. He tilted the hat. It completely covered the cheesy powder. "I'm glad my

head is orange, Darwin. If it weren't, I wouldn't have thought to wear this hat to school."

"The bus is here!" yelled Mrs. Watterson. Gumball and Darwin hurried toward the door. "Good luck!" she called after them.

"I don't need luck," said Gumball, striding out the door. **"I've got a hat!"** He clapped Darwin on his back. "Nothing can go wrong when you're wearing a hat."